About this book

Many children have difficulty puzzling out letters because they
are abstract symbols. Letterland's worldwide success is all about its
enduring characters who give these symbols life and stop them from
being abstract. In this book we meet Dippy Duck. Her story is carefully
designed to emphasise the sounds that the letter 'D' makes in words.
This definitive, original story book is an instant collector's classic,
making learning fun for a new generation of readers.

A TEMPLAR BOOK

This edition published in the UK in 2008 by Templar Publishing
an imprint of The Templar Company plc,
The Granary, North Street, Dorking, Surrey, RH4 1DN, UK
www.templarco.co.uk

First published by Hamlyn Publishing, 1985
Devised and produced by The Templar Company plc

ISBN 978-1-84011-770-7

Printed in China

Classic LETTERLAND
Storybooks

Dippy Duck
Dresses up

Written by
Jane Launchbury & Richard Carlisle

Illustrated by
Jane Launchbury

templar publishing

One day Dippy Duck was having dinner when there was a knock on her Duck Door.

Dippy saw a big, red card appear through her letterbox. It landed on the doormat.

Dippy stopped eating and picked it up. "Dear Dippy," said the card, "please come to a Fancy Dress party tonight!"

Dippy Duck was delighted. She loved dressing up.

Dippy thought and thought about different ways of dressing up.

She thought of dressing up as a donkey, but decided she didn't have enough legs.

She thought of dressing up as a dragon, but decided her tail was too short.

"I will go and look in my dressing up drawer," she decided. "There's bound to be something good in there."

The first thing Dippy found was a pair of dark sun-glasses. She put them on.

Then she found an old hat and an old coat. She put them on too.
She also found a feather duster.
"This will do for a beard," she thought.

When she looked in the mirror, Dippy was delighted with her disguise. "I look just like a detective," she said to herself. "Now all I need is something to cover up my duck feet."

So she dived back into the drawer to find some boots to wear.

Soon it was time to leave for the party. Dippy was very excited as she set off down the path through the woods.

She thought of all the delicious food there would be to eat. That made her hungry.

Then she thought she heard a strange noise. She peered into the darkness of the wood, but there was nothing to be seen.

"Now's my chance to be a real detective," decided Dippy. So she crept through the bushes to take a closer look.

What she found made her rather frightened. Poking out from behind a big bush was a long spiky tail. It was covered in spots and when Dippy poked it, it wriggled from side to side.

"This looks dangerous," thought Dippy. She tried to remember if any of the other animals in Letterland had such a funny tail – but she couldn't think of a single one.

Dippy had to find out more about this strange beast. So she peeked round the bush.

There, standing right in front of her, was a huge animal. It had a long thin neck and a tiny head. All down it's back were big diamond-shaped spines.

There was no doubt about it… it was definitely a DINOSAUR!
Dippy Duck felt dizzy. The dinosaur looked so frightening.

Dippy wondered if dinosaurs ate ducks. "I do hope they don't!" she said to herself.

Dippy Duck was about to run away, when she realised that the dinosaur wasn't alone.

Standing nearby was a donkey with funny legs that seemed to go in different directions… and a doctor with a rather large nose, dressed in a smart white coat.

Dippy Duck began to see more and more rather odd looking people and animals.

There was even a dragon who was trying to hide behind a tree.

Then Dippy Duck saw a big table covered with lots and lots of food. Everyone was helping themselves... even the dinosaur!

At last Dippy realised where she was. This was the Fancy Dress party! It was being held in the woods!

Dippy Duck was most relieved. Now instead of being frightened, she began to wonder who everyone was behind their disguise.

J ust then, the spiky-tailed dinosaur came up to her and said, "We've all decided that we need your help."

"Why me?" asked Dippy Duck. "Because you are a detective!" said the dinosaur. "That means you can help us find out who everyone is!" "Oh," laughed Dippy Duck. "All right!"

Dippy Duck started to look at everyone more closely. She looked at the doctor's face, but she couldn't recognise him. The she looked down at his feet... she was sure she had seen those feet somewhere before. Then she guessed!

"You are the Hairy Hat Man!" she cried. And he was. Then she studied the donkey. What were those golden strands of hair poking out from the donkey's neck? It didn't take Dippy long to work out that the front end of the donkey was Golden Girl and the back end was Naughty Nick.

Soon she had guessed who nearly everyone was, even the terrible looking dragon. She was really the Wicked Witch. There was only one left – the dinosaur… Who could it be?

Dippy thought she knew, but just as she was about to speak, the Hairy Hat Man appeared with all the Fancy Dress prizes.

"Here we have a prize for the best disguise," said the Hairy Hat Man. "I think it should go to the dinosaur because nobody can guess who he is!"

"Wait a minute," yelled Dippy Duck, "I think it's really Eddy Elephant." And sure enough it was. "But he should still get the prize," she added. "Oh thank you," smiled Eddy. "And here's a special prize for you – for being such a good detective."

"How wonderful," said Dippy, and she really was delighted. "Next time there's a Fancy Dress party," she thought to herself, "I shall dress up as a detective again!"

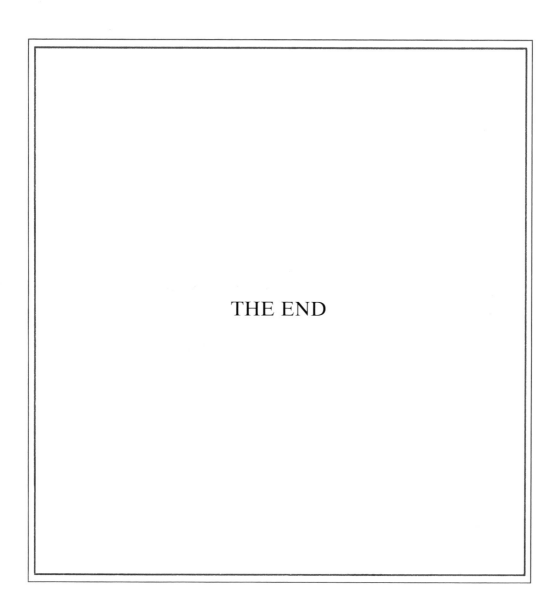

THE END